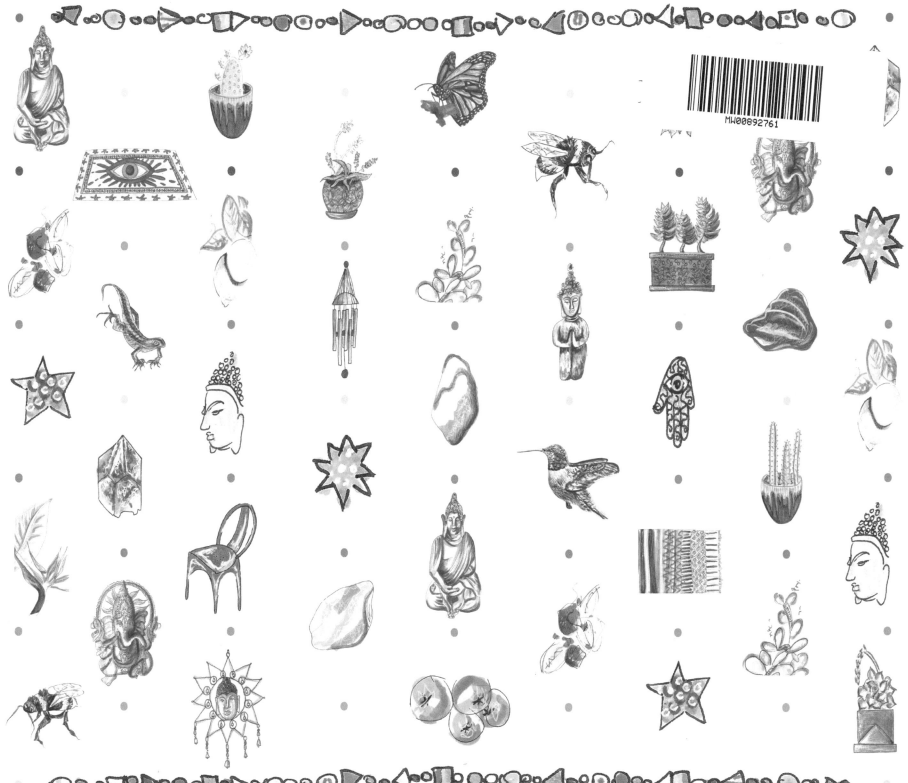

MW00892761

BUMBLEBEE PAPERBACK EDITION
Copyright © Julia Bush 2023
The right of Julia Bush to be identified as author of
this work has been asserted in accordance with sections 77 and 78
of the Copyright, Designs and Patents Act 1988

A CIP catalogue record for this title is
available from the British Library.

ISBN: 978-1-83934-849-5

Bumblebee Books is an imprint of
Olympia Publishers.

First Published in 2023

Bumblebee Books
Tallis House
2 Tallis Street
London
EC4Y 0AB

Printed in Great Britain

My Patio

For Gavin Bear, you are my sunshine   Written and Illustrated by Julia Bush

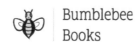

Bumblebee
Books

This is my patio.

It has succulents...

bougainvillea...

jade...

cacti...

and a
loquat tree.

There are Buddha
statues and a Ganesh, too!

Some evil eyes and wind chimes!

I could try to count all the seaglass but I can't count that high, so Mama will help...

One

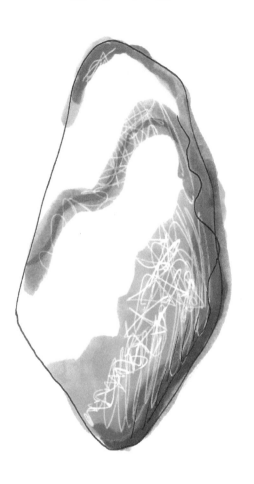

Two

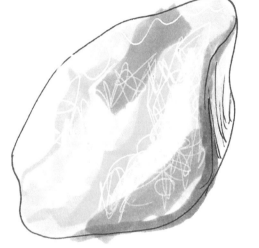

Three

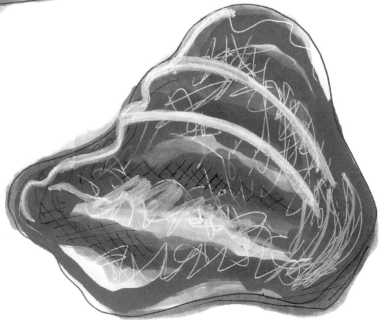

WHAT'S THAT?

A monarch butterfly?

Sometimes I see that butterfly
through the sliding glass doors
while I'm eating lunch inside!

This is my patio.

What do you have where you live?
A window to look through?
Do cars zoom by?

How about
a backyard
with grass?

What about an
herb garden?

Do you live
on a farm?

Does your apartment have a balcony?
What is your view like?

Do you see
an alleyway?

Can you see
mountains?

Animals?
What kinds
of animals?

Buildings?
Stores?

Trees?
Leaves?

Is there a doggy
with a bone?

Or a kitty
sniffing around?

How about a deer
or some bunnies?

Can you see birds
on telephone wires?

In my patio there is a lizard that likes
to sunbathe on our big Buddha statue.

Can you see into your neighbor's home?

can but OOPS - I'll look over here instead and give them some privacy.

Do you live on a
busy street or
near a freeway?

How about in
the suburbs
or in the city?

Maybe your
closest neighbor
is miles away...

WOW!

I can only imagine all the possibilities!

Who has a
pool or jacuzzi?

An ocean?

Can you see a
body of water?
A stream?

I don't! In my patio I see fluffy
clouds and hummingbirds and bees!

I like to imagine what you see because it makes me feel FREE!

Acknowledgments

Thank you
Derek,
Gavin,
the Baby in my belly,
my lovely family,
my delightfully weird friends,
and
anyone who ever gave me
something for my patio.

About the Author

Julia Bush is a Los Angeles-based contemporary artist specializing in oil paints, collage, digital arts, and various other media. Julia holds a Bachelor's degree in Studio Arts, a Master's degree in Education, and seven years of teaching visual arts at the high school level. She is a devoted mother and wife with a toddler and a baby on the way.

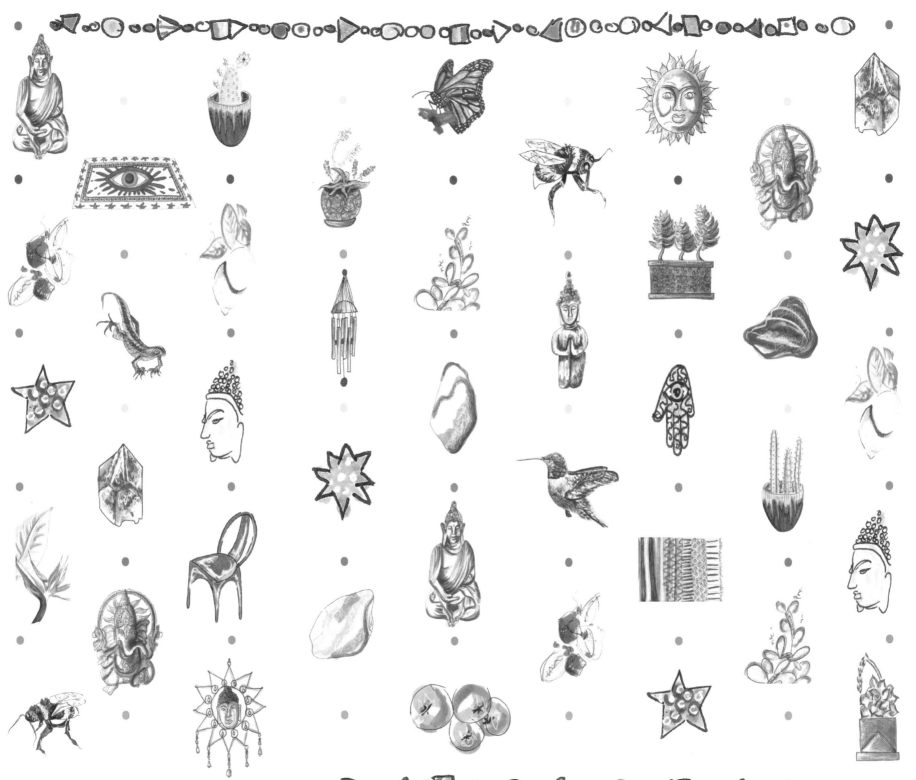

Printed in the USA
CPSIA information can be obtained
at www.ICGtesting.com
LVHW061030281023

762444LV00036B/315